Wizard Tales

Stories of Enchantment and Magic
from Around the World

For Tym, Grand Wizard, with much love – FW
For Roberto, Gianna e la libreria
and Francesca Lazzarato – FN

First published in Great Britain in 2002 by
Pavilion Children's Books
A member of **Chrysalis** Books plc
64 Brewery Road
London N7 9NT
www.pavilionbooks.co.uk

A CIP catalogue record for this book is available
from the British Library.

ISBN 1 84365 008 8

Set in Bernhard Modern and Walbaum MT
Printed in China by C&C Offset

2 4 6 8 10 9 7 5 3

This book can be ordered direct from the publisher. Please contact
the Marketing Department. But try your bookshop first.

WIZARD TALES

Stories of Enchantment and Magic
from Around the World

Retold by Fiona Waters   Illustrated by Fabian Negrin

Pavilion Children's Books

Contents

The Wizard Kaltenbach

A GERMAN TALE OF A CLEVER MAGPIE

The streets of Angleburg were narrow and crooked, and you never quite knew where a side-alley would take you, even if you had lived in the town all your life. The houses were tall and narrow. In some of the darkest alleys you could shake hands with your neighbour across the way merely by leaning out of your window. In one of the oddest-looking of these quaint houses lived Mr Kaltenbach. He was very old and it was widely accepted that he was a wizard, although few knew that his reputation stretched far beyond the tight little streets of Angleburg. Notwithstanding, he was always treated with great respect for no one wished to find themselves suddenly transformed into a toad. People would knock at his door under cover of darkness seeking a remedy for an infestation of rats or a love potion or a cure for warts.

In another part of this curious town lived a poor orphan boy called Wendelin. When a friend kindly offered him an apprenticeship in a weaver's workshop, he declined as he could not bear the thought of sitting all day in a dark cramped room. But as he meandered

11

aimlessly round the streets of Angleburg, he realized that he would have to find work if he was going to survive. Every day he walked the streets looking for work, and one day his wanderings took him to the street where Mr Kaltenbach lived. With a thrill of fear, Wendelin saw the wizard standing on his doorstep.

"You must be hungry, Wendelin," said the wizard in a cold hoarse voice. "Come inside and I will share my supper with you." But Wendelin turned to run away, fear closing his throat in spite of the delicious smells that were coming from inside Mr Kaltenbach's house.

"You have to eat, surely?" muttered the wizard. "Why not come inside and see what I have to say?" and he turned to walk back inside the strange house.

And then, strangest of all, without seeming to have moved, Wendelin found himself inside the house and standing in the most extraordinary room he had ever seen. The walls were covered with great high bookcases which were crammed with piles of ancient leather-bound books. A huge table in the middle of the floor was a jumble of glass phials filled with curiously coloured liquids, parchment scrolls covered in blood-red lettering and a very big black cat with huge unblinking eyes. The wizard clapped his hands and a small monkey scampered in, carrying a wooden tray piled high with delicious food. There was a small roasted chicken, still steaming, a deep dish of buttered potatoes, a golden dish of crystallized fruits, a flask of pure golden wine, and much more besides. Wendelin set to the feast with a will and while he ate the wizard explained what he would like in return for such daily meals. Wendelin was to work in the wizard's garden looking after his herbs and flowers, and as well as his food he would have a bed in the attic and a new suit of clothes.

It seemed a dream come true to Wendelin and he nervously agreed to the wizard's demands. The wizard

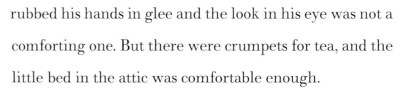

rubbed his hands in glee and the look in his eye was not a comforting one. But there were crumpets for tea, and the little bed in the attic was comfortable enough.

The next day, Wendelin began his work in the garden. The wizard grew all manner of exotic plants, some of which were undoubtedly poisonous. The boy was happy to be out in the fresh air though, and he worked hard all day. Supper was delicious and, as he fell asleep that night, it seemed that he had not made such a bad bargain after all.

The wizard Kaltenbach had many strange visitors, but one in particular always seemed to leave him very agitated. The mysterious guest would arrive late at night, but Wendelin could never quite see who it was.

One morning after the visitor had been, Shackerack, the wizard's pet magpie, called out to Wendelin as he passed by her cage. "Wendelin, you must beware!" croaked the bird. "You are in great danger!"

Wendelin had not even known that Shackerack could talk, but he was very alarmed by her message.

"The invisible guest is Urian, the greatest sorcerer of all. Ten years ago, Mr Kaltenbach sold his soul to him. Kaltenbach's time is nearly up, but he has promised Urian a replacement soul – yours!" said Shackerack. "I can help you, but you have to trust me enough to give me my freedom."

Wendelin decided to trust the bird for she had a bright look in her eye.

"What must I do?" Wendelin asked.

"Let me go, and I will fetch the ring of the great magician Girandola which lies hidden in a great book of spells high on the uppermost shelf of one of the bookcases. Kaltenbach has long since forgotten it is there. With this ring in your possession you are safe from Urian and Kaltenbach, and I am sure you will use it wisely when you too are free. Once I have given you the ring, you must take me out into the garden and set me free."

With trembling fingers, Wendelin opened the cage and Shackerack flew up to the top of the dustiest bookcase. She opened a cobwebby book and Wendelin saw a gleam of gold. She flew back down and, perching on his shoulder, dropped a heavy ring into Wendelin's hand.

"Now, let me go!" she said with a loud crow of triumph, and they ran down the corridor and out into the garden. Shackerack swooped high into the sky and with a harsh cry of delight disappeared from view — just as the wizard appeared by the open door.

"Wicked boy! What have you done?" he shouted and reached for his wand. Muttering incantations, he pointed it at Wendelin but instead of something terrible happening, purple smoke poured out of the wand.

"Ahhh!" shrieked the wizard. "I am undone! You have the ring of Girandola," and he sank to the floor in despair. Wendelin ran out of the house, and did not stop until he had left Angleburg far, far behind him.

That night a terrible noise woke everyone in Angleburg. A fiery light filled the windows of Mr Kaltenbach's house, and a mighty wind blew out of his chimney. The next morning, when the neighbours stepped gingerly over the threshold, they found Mr Kaltenbach lying on the floor, quite dead. Of all his books and potions there was not a sign, and all the plants in the garden were shrivelled. And there were no more late-night visitors to the house ever again.

Far away outside the city, a magnificent castle appeared as if from nowhere. The owner said his name was Wendelin, and all he seemed to want to do was to grow healing herbs and make marvellous potions that could cure any kind of sickness. Everyone loved and trusted him, none more so than the bright-eyed magpie that was always perched on his shoulder.

Glooscap

Glooscap was a powerful medicine man and magician. His fellow tribesmen loved him for he could do anything and was always there to help them. He created all the animals, and made them peaceful creatures who would be useful to humans. He never grew old, but at times his magic powers waned and when this happened he became very vulnerable.

Glooscap lived quietly on an island with his family and his dogs, but on the same island there also lived Win-Pe, an evil sorcerer. Win-Pe was jealous of the great love and admiration that everyone had for Glooscap, and he resolved to destroy the magician.

It was the start of the long dark winter and Glooscap had left the island for a short journey to another tribe who needed his help, leaving his family and dogs behind. He was tired and his magic was at a very low ebb, but he would never let anyone down when they needed him.

Win-Pe saw his chance. He went to Glooscap's camp with some of his men and captured Glooscap's grandmother and his brother and all his dogs. He trampled out the fire and then fled to another island, just as Glooscap was returning.

Glooscap was tired after his journey and his magic was gone, but he saw the direction in which Win-Pe paddled his canoe and he resolved to rescue his family as soon as he could.

He stayed alone on the island, cold and lonely, through the icy winter days and endless nights. Slowly, slowly, Glooscap regained his magic powers until one day he climbed onto a huge rock on the shoreline and began to sing his magic to the waves. His voice carried far, far over the water, and before long a great whale appeared.

"Great whale, please carry me to my family who have been stolen away by the wicked sorcerer, Win-Pe," sang Glooscap.

The whale swam right up to the rock and Glooscap stepped onto its back. The whale swam straight as an arrow, with Glooscap singing all the while astride its back. But as they drew near land, the whale grew fearful that the water wouldn't be deep enough.

"Trust me, great whale, the water is deep enough," sang Glooscap.

On they travelled. The whale grew ever more fearful.

"Great Glooscap, the water is too shallow for me to swim any closer! I shall be stranded," it cried. But Glooscap urged it on, even closer to the shore. With a mighty flip of its tail, the whale made one final surge and then it was stranded on the sand. Glooscap jumped off the whale's back and spoke aloud.

"Noble creature, you have carried me, brave and true, towards my family. I give you a gift that will help your family and their families for ever and ever," and Glooscap passed his magic

pipe of peace to the whale. The whale took a deep breath, and a great spout of water appeared from the top of its head as Glooscap pushed the huge creature back into deeper water so it could swim away to safety. Thereafter, whenever people saw a whale spouting they remembered how Glooscap was carried across the ocean to rescue his family.

Once ashore, Glooscap looked for signs of where his brother and grandmother might have been taken by Win-Pe. Glooscap was a fabled woodsman and tracker, and he could read the tiniest of signs on the ground. He soon found their trail although it was long cold. Thus it was that he found himself crouched behind a fir tree one evening, looking down onto Win-Pe's camp.

He saw his grandmother and brother, both looking thin but still proudly defiant. He heard Win-Pe shouting at them to get supper, and a great anger rose in Glooscap's heart. But he watched and waited, utterly motionless in the gathering darkness.

As dawn broke, Glooscap's brother began collecting firewood. When he drew near to the fir tree, Glooscap hooted three times like a great snowy owl. His brother looked up, delight spreading across his face, for this was their family signal. There was time for no more than a few hurried words, then Glooscap hid again behind the tree. He had told his brother to provoke Win-Pe into losing his temper for then the sorcerer's mind would be filled with anger, driving out all his magic.

Glooscap's brother was as good as his word. Whatever it was that he said, the effect was immediate. The brother came crashing through the trees, Win-Pe in hot pursuit. The sorcerer skidded to a sudden halt when he saw the mighty Glooscap step out from behind the fir tree. In vain, Win-Pe tried to summon his magic powers, but Glooscap just seemed to grow taller and taller, and more and more menacing. Glooscap reached out, a white feather appearing in his hand. He brushed Win-Pe on the shoulder with the feather, and in a great puff of evil-smelling smoke the wicked sorcerer disappeared and was never seen to walk the earth ever again.

Glooscap and his grandmother and his brother and the dogs returned joyfully to their island home. And whoever met Glooscap on the way was forever wiser and happier, so great was the medicine man's magic.

The Green Man

There was once a miller who was looking at his mill-wheel one day, when something down by the water's edge caught his eye. It was a tiny green man. His hair was a mass of tangled moss, his skin smooth as birch bark and he wore a cloak of oak leaves. The miller had heard tales of the magical powers of such creatures, so he bent down gently as if to speak to him, but then grasped hold of the little green man.

The little green man cried out in distress, but the miller held fast to his prize. He carried him indoors and locked him in a glass box. Soon, the villagers came flocking, and the wily miller charged everyone a penny to view the green man. Now there was no need for the miller to grind corn any more. But the little green man became thin, his bright eyes grew dim and his oak-leaf cloak faded to a dull brown.

One day, the miller's son looked closely at the little green man imprisoned in the glass box, and saw two tears roll down his cheeks. "Why are you crying, little man?" he asked. "You look very fine in your glass box."

23

"I cannot bear being shut in like this," replied the little green man. "I want to feel the good brown earth beneath my feet, the wind in my hair and the dew on my face."

The miller's son understood. Without further thought he unlocked the box. The little green man sprang to the window and called out, "Come with me! We shall live under the trees and I shall teach you the secrets of nature!"

And so it happened. The miller's son and the little green man were never again seen in the village. The lazy miller had to return to grinding corn and he seemed forever to be dogged by misfortune. But the little green man was as good as his word and the miller's son grew into a fine young man, well versed in the ways of the wild creatures and plants.

Time passed and one day, years later, the little green man said to the miller's son, "I have taught you all I know of my world. It is time for you to seek your fortune. You must go to the king's palace to find work, but you must not speak one word or you will be undone. Should you ever be in trouble, however, find three oak leaves and rub them together, and I shall be there by your side in a twinkling."

And so the young man set off. Long before he reached the palace everyone was roaring with laughter at him for he looked very odd. His hair was long and tangled and full of leaves. He wore no shoes and his clothes were faded and tattered. But he had an honest face, so the cook took him into the kitchen and set him to washing the mountains of dirty dishes that were piled up everywhere after a banquet the night before. The young man did not like working in the hot steamy kitchen and he was always dropping plates, so he did not last long there. But, as luck would have it, the stable boy had just run away and so the young man found himself at work in the palace stables, grooming the king's horses.

One day, he heard the king talking to the head groom. "The Duke of Ravencourt has declared war. He is marching towards the town even now and I am very much afraid he will defeat us, we are so outnumbered."

The young man admired the king and did not want him defeated. How could he help? Then he remembered the words of the little green man. He found an oak tree and rubbed three leaves together. Faster than the twinkling of an eye, there stood the little green man.

"Close your eyes and turn around twice, and you shall see how I help you!"

The young man did as he was bid and found himself in full armour, seated on a huge war horse at the head of a great troop of men. They galloped out of the palace gates and when the Duke of Ravencourt saw the mighty army, he turned and fled. The king was delighted, but when he went to thank the strange young knight he was nowhere to be seen.

After this excitement, the young man found it difficult to settle down to scrubbing out stables and before long the head groom found another stable boy. But again luck was with the miller's son. The palace gardener was getting old and stiff, so he was delighted to have someone to help with all the weeding and digging.

Now the young man was truly happy as he was able to use all the secrets he had learnt from the little green man. The gardens had never looked lovelier. The princess would come to look at the tumbling roses that cascaded over the ancient palace walls, and before long she spotted the young man working away diligently. She spoke to him, but, although he smiled, never a word did he utter. The princess was perplexed. Every day, the young man cut roses for her to wear in her hair, and sweet honeysuckle to perfume her room, and lavender to strew in her bath, but he remained ever silent.

A year passed and the king's thoughts returned to the strange knight who had saved him from the Duke of Ravencourt. He sent messengers all over the kingdom asking the knight to come to court. But he did not. Then the king announced that if the knight would present himself he could marry the princess. So sure was the king that this would persuade the knight to come that he invited everyone to the wedding and ordered the kitchens to prepare a great feast. He gave the princess a golden casket that she was to present to the knight when he arrived.

The feast was magnificent and the guests had a splendid day, but of the mysterious knight there was no sign. The princess was not too worried, if the truth were to be told, for she had fallen in love with the silent young gardener. That evening, she went to the garden, where she found the young man. She thrust the golden casket into his hands, then fled without daring to look at his face.

27

Just as dawn was breaking, the little green man suddenly appeared in the garden. He carried a magnificent green velvet suit, embroidered with golden oak leaves. Outside, there was a company of soldiers, all with golden trumpets around their necks.

The young man put on the suit and went with the soldiers to the palace gates. The soldiers lifted the trumpets and blew a ringing blast that brought the king, wearing only his nightshirt, to the balcony. When he saw his mysterious knight in the courtyard, he ran to fetch the princess. She was overjoyed when she saw that the knight holding the golden casket was none other than her silent gardener. The little green man appeared suddenly yet again and he told the young man his vow of silence was over.

After a great deal of talking (the princess and the young man had a great deal to say to each other) they were married, and everyone lived happily ever after.

The Sorcerer Kaldoon

A TALE OF WICKEDNESS FROM TRANSYLVANIA

There was once a farmer called Viktor, who fell on bad times. All he had left in the world were his good wife, Maria, and Anna, his beautiful daughter. The cupboards were bare, the barns empty, and only feathers lay in the chicken coops. So Viktor set off on the long walk to town, where he hoped to find work.

It was a long way. Viktor walked and walked, and then he walked some more. As night fell he came upon a village. Following the sound of laughter and music, an astonishing sight met his eyes. In the village square, fiddlers were playing as if their lives depended on it, and everyone was whirling about in a wild dance. Great wooden tables were piled high with all manner of food and drink. And at the heart of it all a handsome young man was throwing golden coins everywhere! Viktor thought they must all be mad, and he turned to creep away.

"Not so fast, my friend!" shouted the handsome man. "I have been expecting you. I know you have fallen on hard times," and he thrust a handful of gold into the farmer's shaking hands.

"I am Prince Kaldoon and I can help you. All I ask is the hand of your fair Anna whose beauty is greater than all the golden lilies in the meadow!"

Well, Viktor was very taken aback at this. But he felt the weight of the gold in his hands and he saw the tables groaning with food, and Prince Kaldoon was very handsome… It did not take him long to stuff the gold into his pockets, to pile a great platter with food – and to promise his daughter in marriage to the smiling prince. But he failed to notice that Prince Kaldoon's smile did not reach his eyes.

The next day, when Viktor awoke, he had to pinch himself to see if he was still dreaming. He was lying in a huge four-poster bed, wearing the most richly embroidered clothes, and a uniformed servant was offering him a cup of hot chocolate. Prince Kaldoon appeared as if from nowhere.

"Good morning, my friend! You must be up and on your way. Go home and tell Maria and Anna of your good fortune. I will send a coach to collect you all for the wedding in seven days time," and he hustled the dazed farmer out of the door.

Once back at the farm, Viktor happily told Maria and Anna about their great change in fortune. But when he came to the part about Anna marrying Prince Kaldoon, he was dismayed to find Anna was not at all keen. Aside from the fact that she greatly resented being given away in this casual manner, she had secretly given her heart to Florian, their neighbour's son.

But Viktor was not about to let his daughter's fancies get in the way of his new fortune, so he ignored her tears and pleading and thought only of spending Prince Kaldoon's gold. He chose fine clothes and leather boots for himself and Maria. He bought cows and horses for the farm, and hired men to plough the fields.

Soon the seven days were up, and Prince Kaldoon's coach arrived to collect Viktor and Maria and, of course, the reluctant bride. By now she looked a perfect fright. Her eyes were red from weeping, her cheeks were puffy, her hair looked like a bird's nest, and her nails were bitten to the quick. She certainly did not look anything like the golden lilies in the meadow!

Prince Kaldoon was waiting inside the palace gates as the coach arrived. He wore a flowing golden cloak and a richly jewelled crown glittered on his head. "Where is my bride, the beautiful Anna?" he called. A dishevelled figure stumbled out of the coach. Prince Kaldoon's face darkened with anger.

"Is this how you repay my generosity?" he demanded, glaring at Viktor. "You have made a great mistake in tricking me." Prince Kaldoon grabbed Anna and threw her over the saddle of a great black horse. He jumped up behind her and they galloped off in a clatter of hooves. Maria fainted clean away and Viktor wrung his hands in despair.

Then a strong voice by Viktor's side said, "Do not despair, Viktor. I will rescue Anna." It was Florian, who had secretly followed them on horseback. He loved Anna with all his heart and had promised to protect her ever since she had told him of her father's unwise pledge to Kaldoon. "He is no prince, but a wicked sorcerer. She is in great danger and I must go after them with the speed of light," and he too galloped off in pursuit of the great black horse.

Ahead of Florian, Anna clung to the black horse's mane, absolutely terrified. Kaldoon just laughed and spurred the horse on even faster. They came to a deep ravine with steep rocky sides. Far, far below rushed a fierce river, but, to Anna's horror, Kaldoon urged the horse over the edge! "Now you see who I am, Anna! I am the Sorcerer Kaldoon and this ravine is to be your home."

Florian dashed up a few moments later and looked in horror at the deep ravine. How could his precious Anna have survived such a fall? Then, as he looked carefully, Florian saw that it might be possible to find a few precarious footholds down the sides. He tied his horse to a tree, wound a rope round his shoulder and started the terrifying climb down.

Many times his foot slipped, but on he struggled until he reached the bottom. It was as dark as night down there, but the light of one small candle glowed up ahead. Florian crept towards the light as quietly as a mouse. The candle was burning on a rocky shelf deep inside a cave and there, huddled on the floor, was Anna! Of the Sorcerer Kaldoon, there was no sign. Florian called softly to Anna who could not believe her eyes when she saw who was standing there.

The climb back up was one of pure terror for Anna. Florian had tied her firmly to his waist with the rope, and told her to close her eyes as he inched slowly up the steep sides of the ravine, his precious burden held close. By now, he was desperately tired as well as fearful of falling, but somehow they made it to the top where his faithful horse was waiting. Anna and Florian journeyed home in utter happiness at their escape, and both quite readily forgave Viktor when they saw how truly sorry he was that his greed and selfishness had so nearly cost his daughter's life. Anna and Florian were married as soon as possible, and from that day on they all lived in great contentment.

And what of Kaldoon? He had been fast asleep, deep in the cave, on a huge pile of gold coins. When he awoke in the morning to find Anna gone, he was so very angry that he burst into flames, and soon there was nothing left of him and all his evil but a pile of grey ash.

Tall, Broad and Keen

For many years, all the king had wanted was to see his only son, Prince Karel, marry and settle down. One morning over breakfast, the king said, "My son, take this golden key and go to the top of the North Tower of the castle. There you will find a door which you should open. Go inside and you will see what you will see."

Prince Karel was very puzzled by his father's directions. He could not remember ever seeing a door at the top of the North Tower. But sure enough, there at the top of the winding staircase was the door. The golden key fitted the lock smoothly and Prince Karel stepped down into a circular room.

Twelve great windows rose from the floor to the ceiling — which was midnight blue and covered with glittering stars. The windows were of stained glass and the sunlight passing through the brilliant colours of the panes fell in pools on the polished marble floor. Prince Karel saw that every window portrayed a princess, each more beautiful than the last.

And as he looked, the figures of the princesses began to move as if they were alive, and they all smiled, gazing down at the bemused prince.

One window alone was covered by a heavy dark velvet curtain. When Prince Karel drew the curtain back there was another princess. She was dressed all in silver and white with a crown of tiny pearls on her long dark hair. She was lovelier than all the others could ever be, but she looked pale and sad, and she was not smiling. The prince drew in his breath sharply – here was his dream princess! But as he reached out his hand towards the window, the room grew dark, there was a sudden clap of thunder and all the princesses disappeared.

Prince Karel dashed down the stairs of the tower to look for his father. When the king heard about the sad princess, his eyes filled with tears.

"Alas, my son," he said. "You have chosen the Princess Katya. She is shut up in the fortress of an evil wizard many, many leagues from here. Go with my blessing and seek her out. She shall be yours if you keep a steadfast heart!"

And so Prince Karel set off to find the Princess Katya. He rode for many days and nights without stopping, through forests and over marshes and round great lakes. He had stopped to let his horse take a drink from a deep pool when he heard a voice behind him.

"Young sir! If you take me with you it will be to your benefit."

Prince Karel turned round and there, hurrying towards him, was the tallest man he had ever seen.

"Who are you?" asked the prince, "And why should I take you with me?"

"My name is Tall and I can stretch as far as your eyes can see."

"Well, that sounds useful," murmured Prince Karel. "Come with me then," and they set off together.

After a while, Tall said, "Young sir! Will you not take my friend Broad with you too?"

"Who is he, and why should I take him with me?" asked the prince.

"Here I am, sir," said a jolly voice by his side, and when Prince Karel turned to look there was a very short round man who looked rather like a barrel.

"I can swallow the deepest ocean or the mightiest wind," said Broad.

"Well, that sounds useful," murmured Prince Karel. "Come with me then," and they set off together.

After a while, Tall said, "Young sir! Will you not take my friend Keen with you too?"

"Who is he, and why should I take him with me?" asked the prince.

"Here I am, sir," said a high, thin voice by his side, and when Prince Karel turned to look there was a man with a scarf bound tightly over his eyes.

"My eyesight is so powerful that I can see through anything," said Keen.

"Well, that sounds useful," murmured Prince Karel. "Come with me then," and they all set off together.

As they walked, Prince Karel explained his quest for Princess Katya. Keen took off his scarf, revealing a pair of incredibly pale blue eyes. He looked all about, through a great hill, over a dark forest and under a deep lake.

"I see the princess," he cried. "The wizard's fortress is a few more leagues from here, we must travel due north."

And so away they sped as fast as ever possible.

Just as dusk was falling, they arrived at the wizard's gloomy fortress. It looked very forbidding, and Prince Karel was glad of his three companions as they crossed the drawbridge. They walked down a long corridor until they reached a huge banqueting hall with a blazing fire at one end. The room was filled with richly dressed lords and ladies, none of whom seemed to notice the newcomers. As Prince Karel looked around the room, he realized with a sudden chill that all the lords and ladies were not moving because they had been turned to stone.

With a crash, a door opened at the far end of the hall. There stood the wizard, dressed from head to toe in swirling blood-red silk. He led by the hand a most beautiful girl, dressed all in silver and white with a crown of tiny pearls on her long dark hair. She looked pale and sad, and she was not smiling.

The wizard's eyes glittered with malice as he saw Prince Karel. "Well, young man, here is the princess whom you seek to take away from me!" he said, and his voice was like the hiss of a snake.

Prince Karel smiled at the princess and tried to talk to her, but she stood as if carved from marble. Not a word did she speak.

"She shall be yours if you can find where I have hidden her before daybreak. But if you fail, you and your strange companions will be turned to stone," and the wizard looked down his long nose at Tall, Broad and Keen before striding out of the hall, taking the princess with him.

40

The prince and his new friends looked at each other in dismay. They were all exhausted and although they really needed to start looking for the princess right away, they slumped together on a deep couch by the fire for a moment. But, of course, this was their undoing. Soon their eyes drooped and finally closed as sleep quite overtook them all, even Prince Karel himself. They slept so deeply you might have wondered if there was not some enchantment in the air. Just as the first light of dawn crept over the far distant mountains, the prince awoke with a start. Where was the princess? With a great cry of grief he woke Tall, Broad and Keen.

"Fear not, Prince, we shall find her for you," said Tall.

Keen tore off his scarf and looked out of the window. "I see her! The wizard has tied her to the topmost branches of a tall, tall tree on an island in the middle of a wide, wide lake. Come, my friends, to the rescue!" he cried.

Tall picked Keen and Broad up in his arms and strode off down the road, his great strides covering ten leagues at every pace. As soon as they reached the wide, wide lake, Broad lay down on the shore and began to drink. He drank and drank without pause and soon all the water was gone. Tall strode to the middle of the island and gently picked the princess out of the topmost branches of the tall, tall tree.

Keen looked back towards the fortress. "Hurry, my friend Tall! The wizard has woken up and is coming down the stairs towards the great hall!" he cried.

And so Tall turned — Keen on his shoulders, the princess under his right arm and Broad clinging to his left arm — and ran as fast as he could towards the fortress.

Prince Karel, in the meantime, was in a state of complete despair. He could hear the wizard trampling downstairs, yet there was no sign of his friends and, most important of all, no sign of the beautiful Princess Katya. And then suddenly there they were, just as the wizard appeared at the door. When he saw Princess Katya standing there, Prince Karel by her side with his sword drawn, the wizard gave a great howl of rage and turned into a huge inky-black raven. He flew out of the window and was never seen again.

Then several things happened at once. The princess blushed and started to thank the prince and his companions for rescuing her, and to explain how she had been captured by the wizard in the first place. The lords and ladies all came back to life, and servants appeared with great platters of food and flagons of wine. When everyone had eaten and drunk their fill, all the talking began again. Prince Karel explained how he would never have succeeded in finding and rescuing the Princess Katya if it hadn't been for his friends, the remarkable Tall and Broad and Keen. He begged them to come home with him and Princess Katya but all three agreed that their work for the prince and princess was done, and so they set off once again to wander the land. And as far as I know they are wandering still.

The Enchanted Soup

A TALE OF MAGIC FROM GERMANY

L ong ago, in an old market town, there lived a poor cobbler with his wife and their son, Hans. Hans always had a ready smile, and when he was not busy helping his father in the workshop, he would keep his mother company as she sold her home-grown vegetables from a stall in the cobbled market place.

One day, a strange old woman stopped by the stall. She had piercing eyes and a long pointed nose and her face was as wrinkled as a prune.

"Are these vegetables fresh?" she demanded, and her voice was as sharp as a midnight cat's.

"Of course they're fresh," said Hans, as the old woman rummaged her way round the neat piles of carrots and potatoes and onions.

Hans' mother grasped him by the sleeve and nudged him to one side.

"I picked them myself this morning," she said cheerfully, offering the old woman a fine bunch of carrots. She did not wish to offend a potential customer.

"Pah!" sneered the old woman. "My donkey finds better carrots than that by the wayside!" She threw the carrots down disdainfully.

Hans was furious. He knew his mother's vegetables were the best in the market place.

"These are the best carrots you will find here today," shouted an angry Hans. "If you do not wish to buy them, be off with you!"

"Very well, my fine young sir, I will buy your mother's vegetables, but you must help me take them home," said the woman. "I live over the bridge, on the other side of the river."

Hans picked up the laden basket and set off behind the old woman. They walked through the market and down the busy lane that led to the bridge. They crossed the river. Hans was surprised to find himself in a street that he did not recognize, although he knew the town like the back of his hand. Then the old woman stopped suddenly in front of a dark building and, opening the door with a great heavy key, pushed Hans and his basket of vegetables inside.

To his astonishment, Hans found himself in a large hall with richly embroidered rugs on the marble floor and heavy velvet curtains at the windows which looked over a marvellous garden. The walls were covered in old paintings and a glittering chandelier lit up the ceiling. As Hans looked round in amazement, a door opened at the end of the hall and a plump little pig wearing a blue and white apron dashed up to the fireplace and placed another log on the fire. Another little pig, also wearing an apron, scuttled up to Hans and, with a courteous bow, seized the basket of vegetables. A white goose then appeared, carrying a bowl of soup which she placed on a table in front of Hans. The goose wore a red ribbon round her neck, a red apron and tiny red shoes.

"You must eat some of my soup before you go back to your mother," said the old woman. "It is delicious — you will see why I insist on the best vegetables."

Hans was not hungry but he felt he had better humour the old woman, and he was curious to see if the goose and the pigs would appear again. So he took a spoonful of the soup, and then another. He had never tasted anything so delicious. He supped up the whole plate, scarcely pausing for breath. The old woman watched him intently and, as he finished, gave a great cackle of laughter. To his horror, Hans felt himself shrinking, smaller and smaller, until he was no bigger than his soup spoon! The little boy leapt off his stool and the old woman chased him into the kitchen and shut the door with a bang.

The two pigs and the goose appeared by his side and told him that a similar thing had happened to them. One of the pigs had been a butcher who had carried home the old woman's meat, the other had been a cook at the royal palace. The poor goose was none other than the princess herself who had been missing from the palace for several months.

Hans promised them that he would do his very best to release them all from the terrible spell the old woman had cast over them — at least he still had his human form. The goose princess told him that the old woman's magic soup was made with a special herb that grew in a dank corner of the garden.

For days, Hans watched and waited, and waited and watched some more. Finally, one day, the old woman left the door ajar long enough for him to slip out into the garden while she was looking the other way. He found the herb and quickly picked a sprig and, holding it tightly in his hand, he set off back to the town.

It was a dangerous journey for one so tiny. Several times people nearly trod on him and once he was cornered by a great barking dog, but somehow or other he made it and soon he was crossing the bridge and trotting into the market place. His mother gave a great shriek when she saw her tiny son, but he soon managed to calm her enough to tell her the whole story. She popped him in her apron pocket for safety and went to find her husband.

"We must take our son to the palace at once," said the cobbler. "I have heard the queen is in a complete decline since the princess disappeared. It will be wonderful to give her good news!"

So the good couple set off, Hans still safely in his mother's pocket. Of course, no one would believe their story when they reached the palace and the guards had just begun to look very fierce when the royal doctor appeared.

"What is all this hubbub?" he demanded. "I must have complete quiet for the queen."

The cobbler heard this and waved frantically to the doctor, calling out, "Sir! Sir! I think I can help you. At least, my son can!"

Fortunately, the doctor was at his wits' end as to how to cure the queen and he was prepared to grasp at anything. His eyebrows rose as he heard the cobbler's tale, and rose even further at the sight of Hans. But he wasted no time in summoning the royal carriage and then he and the king (who had appeared to see what all the fuss was about) and the cobbler

and his wife and Hans all dashed away down the narrow streets and over the bridge. But only Hans could see the road that led to the old woman's house.

"There is obviously a very strong enchantment here," murmured the doctor.

When they arrived in front of the tall dark building, Hans' mother opened the door cautiously. There were the pigs, there was the goose princess and there was the old woman! She gave a great yell and stepped forward to grab Hans but he ran under her feet and, as he did so, touched her foot with the herb. There was a great flash of green light, a huge cloud of black smoke and a very nasty smell — and the old woman vanished utterly, never to be seen again.

Hans then touched the pigs with the magic herb, and there appeared a plump cook complete with chef's hat, and a thin-faced butcher wearing a blue and white striped apron. Hans touched the white goose, and there was the princess, dressed all in white with red roses in her hair. Finally, the princess waved the magic sprig over little Hans and he too was restored to his old self.

Everyone squashed into the royal carriage and raced back to the palace. As soon as she saw the princess, the queen leapt out of bed and danced round the room in sheer delight. The king ordered everyone in the town to come to a huge feast. The cook was kept very busy and, of course, the butcher and the cobbler's wife supplied all the meat and vegetables!

The King of the Warlocks

Long ago, Hamish the fisherman lived with his wife Catriona in a simple cottage by the edge of the sea. He would go out every day in his small boat, and then Catriona would sell the silver herring at market. One day, when Hamish went to pull in his net, he found it curiously heavy. There, in amongst the jumping fish, lay a narrow wooden box and, when Hamish opened it, he found a little boy lying there apparently unharmed by his journey. He rushed back home to Catriona who soon had the child washed and dressed.

"Husband, we must keep this child and look after him as if he were our own. He has obviously been cast out to sea and it is our good fortune that he has landed in your net," she said. And so they kept the little boy and named him Calum.

Many years passed and Calum grew into a fine young man, much loved by his foster parents. Hamish taught him to fish and the two would go out in the boat together every day, except Sunday. Hamish would dig his potatoes on the Sabbath while Calum wandered round the harbour looking at all the ships coming and going.

One day, when Calum was about seventeen, a strange ship arrived in the harbour. The sails were the purest white and the mast was carved and richly gilded. On the deck there stood a tall proud-looking man. He was dressed all in black velvet and his dark eyes glittered. In his hands he held three silver balls, each ringed with sharp spikes. As Calum looked on, spellbound, the stranger tossed the balls high in the air and juggled them so fast that they spun in a blur — and all without cutting his hands on the silver spikes. Calum was entranced and, noticing his interest, the stranger stepped down off the boat, the balls whirling and flashing all the while.

"You like my tricks, Calum?" murmured the stranger.

Calum did not pause to wonder how he knew his name.

"Oh yes!" he replied. "I would love to be able to do that."

"But you can," said the stranger. "Take me to your parents, I will make a deal with them."

When Hamish and Catriona explained how they had discovered Calum, the stranger appeared greatly interested. For, all unbeknownst to Hamish and Catriona, he was a powerful wizard and he realized that Calum must be a fairy child.

"Lend me your son for a year and a day, and I will teach him the art of juggling. Then, when he returns, he will be able to earn much more money than he does as a fisherman," he promised.

Hamish and Catriona only wanted the best for Calum and so they let him sail away on the strange ship with their blessing. As promised, a year and a day later the stranger brought Calum back. And Calum had learnt so well that he stood juggling not three silver spiked balls but seven. He never dropped a single one, and neither did the spikes cut his hands.

"You see how clever your son is!" laughed the stranger. "Let me have him for another year and a day, and I will make him the finest juggler in the world."

And so Calum set off again, but this time, when the year and the day was up, there was no sign of the great ship. After several days of anxious waiting, Hamish and Catriona decided some mischief had befallen Calum and so Hamish set off to look for him. He had absolutely no idea where to begin, so he just followed his nose through dark forests and over deep rivers, but never a trace of Calum did he find. He grew weary of heart and his back and legs ached. One night, as darkness fell, he saw a light glimmering through the trees, and soon he found himself standing in front of a tumbledown cottage. Smoke curled up from the chimney and a candle flickered in the deep-set window.

Hamish knocked on the door. A thin and quavery voice bid him enter. An ancient old man sat in a high settle by a fire. His face was crisscrossed with wrinkles, and a pair of startlingly blue eyes looked kindly at Hamish.

"Come in and welcome, you still have a long journey ahead of you," the old man said. He rose and fetched oatcakes and a honeycomb and a mug of ale. When Hamish felt sufficiently restored, he told the old man about his quest.

"Without doubt your son is in the evil hands of the King of the Warlocks," said the old man. "This is not good, not good at all, but I will help you all I can. Rest for now, and we will talk further in the morning," and so saying, he gave Hamish a warm plaid to wrap himself up in by the fireside.

In the morning, the old man gave Hamish a steaming bowl of porridge and directions to the castle where the King of the Warlocks lived. "Once you reach the castle — and you cannot mistake it, so dreary and gloomy a place it is — you must ask to see the King of the Warlocks. When you meet him you must demand your son back as the time for his safe return has passed. The king will take you to his loft where there will be fourteen pigeons. He will tell you that if you recognize your son you may have him back. The pigeons will all look identical, but do not despair. Calum is the one with a tiny black feather on its head. Choose that one and you will have your son back."

Hamish thanked the old man with all his heart and set off to the castle. It was as the old man had foretold. The castle stood on top of a hill, with many towers and turrets rising grimly into the sky. Hamish pulled the great iron bell pull and when the door creaked open he demanded to see the King of the Warlocks. In a trice, the stranger in the black suit appeared in the doorway. Hamish's knees turned to water as he realized this was the King of the Warlocks.

The king was not pleased to see Hamish and offered him all kinds of gifts to go away, but eventually, with an unpleasant laugh, he took him up into one of the turrets. There were the fourteen pigeons. "Choose the right one and you will have your precious son back," snarled the king with an evil smile.

You can imagine his rage when Hamish picked out the one with the tiny black feather on its head. In the twinkling of an eye there stood Calum, looking none the worse for his adventures.

"Get out of my sight," roared the King of the Warlocks. "And my curse goes with you!"

Hamish and Calum pelted down the stairs, out of the castle and down the hill as fast as their legs would carry them. They stopped by the tumbledown cottage to thank the old man for his help and then made their way home where Catriona was waiting anxiously.

Calum never wanted to travel far from home after this. But the King of the Warlocks had indeed taught him many fantastic tricks and feats of juggling, and people came from far and wide to see the young man whose hands moved so fast they were impossible to follow. The silver balls with the spikes flew high in the air and never a one did Calum drop. Hamish fished for pleasure now, and the family lived together in great contentment for many years. The strange ship with the sails of purest white, and the richly carved and gilded mast was never seen again, but on windy evenings the villagers would scare themselves to bed with the story of the King of the Warlocks.

The Golden Carnation

AN OLD FAIRY TALE FROM ITALY

Many moons ago, a wealthy merchant lived in Italy with his three daughters. The elder two daughters were sour and bitter like lemons, but the youngest was as sweet and pretty as a peach. As he set out on a long voyage to the Spice Islands, the merchant asked each of his daughters what gifts they would like him to bring back.

"A dress covered in tiny golden bells," said the eldest, Maria.

"Silver slippers with glass heels," said the middle daughter, Lucia.

(No 'please' and 'thank you' as I'm sure you have noticed.)

"And what would you like, my dear Florita?" said the merchant, turning to the youngest.

"I would only like you to come home safely, Father," she replied with a smile.

"But your sisters have made special requests; I would not leave you out," said the merchant.

"Very well, Father. I would like a golden carnation, please, and I would like you to come home safely!" she said, laughing.

The merchant set sail the very next day and many weeks later reached port. He met many traders and soon the hold of the ship was groaning with the weight of all the rare and precious spices he had bought. Determined to return home on the next tide, he set off to find the presents for his daughters. In the bazaar he found great lengths of silk, all covered with tiny golden bells, and a dark-eyed tailor who promised to have the dress ready by dawn.

In the leather market he found a cobbler whose stitches were so minute as to be invisible, and he too promised to have the silver slippers with glass heels ready by dawn. But nowhere was there a golden carnation to be found. The merchant searched the flower market and he searched the goldsmiths' vaults and he asked every trader he met but no one could help, so the merchant set sail on the early morning tide. The dress with the tiny golden bells lay in tissue paper in a sandalwood box. The silver slippers with glass heels were in a velvet drawstring bag, all lined with silk. But he had no golden carnation for Florita.

The ship had a safe passage, but it was with a heavy heart that the merchant stepped ashore once again. Where was he to find a golden carnation? He walked aimlessly away from the bustling harbour and, after a while, found himself in a completely unfamiliar wood. He looked around, greatly puzzled. He did not recognize a single landmark. Then, ahead, he saw a great

gateway with huge statues either side of the pathway and filled with curiosity he stepped

inside. The air seemed to crackle with magic and he knew he had somehow wandered into

a garden of deep enchantment. And then, there in front of him, grew a great bush covered

with golden carnations!

Without thinking, the merchant stepped forward and broke off one of the gorgeous

blooms. Instantly, there was a huge flash of purple light and a roll of thunder, and there

stood a mighty wizard. And he looked very cross indeed.

"Who are you, impudent man, and how dare you pick one of my precious carnations?"

he asked, and his eyes flashed with anger.

Haltingly, the merchant explained about his promise to Florita. The wizard scowled.

"As you have picked the carnation you may have it for your daughter, but as payment for

this you must bring your daughter here in three days. If you do not, it will be the worse for

you and all your family," said the wizard, before disappearing in a whirl of smoke.

57

When the merchant arrived home he gave his daughters their presents. The elder two rushed off to try on their gifts, but Florita could see that her father was worried about something.

Eventually the merchant poured out the whole story.

Florita was quite undismayed. "Well, Father, you must take me to meet this wizard tomorrow before he becomes any crosser," she said. "I shall go and pack a few things to take with us."

The next day they set off, the merchant not even quite sure how to find the wizard again, but somehow, just by wishing it, they found themselves in the enchanted garden. Just as suddenly as before, the wizard appeared.

"Well, Florita, to pay for your golden carnation you must stay here and look after my garden. I shall visit you every evening and we will dine together," and so saying, the wizard vanished again.

The merchant was heartbroken, but Florita told him she was quite happy to look after such a lovely garden. He went sadly back to Maria and Lucia, who were still so sour they were not at all sorry to see the back of their lovely younger sister.

Many days passed. Florita greatly enjoyed looking after the garden and began to look forward to her evenings with the wizard, who was not so terrifying once she got to know him. But after a while, she began to worry about her father. She was sure her selfish sisters would not be looking after him properly, and she missed him. She asked the wizard if she might go home for a few days, and at first he refused to let her go. But as she grew quieter and unhappier, he relented.

"I can see you are unhappy so I will let you return, but you must promise to come back in three days or it will be the worse for us both," and he looked sad as he sent her on her way in a golden carriage.

When Florita arrived home, her worst fears were realized. Her father looked ill, the house was a shambles and her sisters only said by way of greeting, "Oh, good! You can tidy the house and get us some supper. We can't find a thing!"

She made her father a bowl of good hot soup and set to the task of cleaning the house. She scrubbed and polished from top to bottom, looking after her father all the while. The three days slipped by without her noticing, and it was only when her father asked whether the golden carnations were still blooming in the wizard's garden that she remembered her promise. In great distress, Florita dashed out of the house. The golden carriage had disappeared and she had to walk through the night, alone and greatly afraid of what the wizard might say. Just as dawn was breaking, she reached the great gates.

But what had happened to the beautiful garden? Huge weeds and brambles were crushing the rare plants and flowers. There was no water in the fountains and the leafy trees drooped sadly. At the foot of the terrace steps, the wizard lay in a crumpled heap. His gorgeous robes were dusty and torn, and his eyes were closed.

Florita knelt by his side and whispered, "What have I done? I only stayed to help my father. I did mean to return to you," and she bent forward and kissed his cheek. Immediately, there was a shower of golden light, full of glittering stars, and there, instead of a great wizard, stood a rather ordinary but very pleasant-looking young man.

"Well, that was a close thing!" he said. "My name is Pietro and I have been under a spell which could only be broken by an act of kindness. Will you stay with me, Florita, and help me look after the garden?" Florita was delighted, but first she collected her father so they could all live together. As for her two sisters, they couldn't abide all the pollen from the flowers in the garden so they had to remain at home looking after each other which, of course, made them more sour than ever!

The Witch in the Stone Boat

A CHILLING TALE FROM ICELAND

Long, long ago, when the winter winds blew icy cold from the north, there lived a king and queen who had a son called Sigurd. He was a mighty warrior but he had a kind heart. The king was growing old and frail and it was his great desire that Sigurd should have a wife by his side when he came to rule after him. The king had a fine girl in mind, Princess Gullveig, but she lived in another kingdom, far across the seas. Sigurd was happy to embark on this quest for his bride and so he set off to sail for several weeks until he reached the shores of Gullveig's home.

Sigurd's father had made a fine choice in Gullveig. She was not only beautiful, but she was courteous and gentle, and she possessed a quiet determination which, as you will see, was to stand her in good stead.

Sigurd and Gullveig were married and in time they had a child, a son whom they called Agnar. He was a happy child and he never cried or fretted.

News came that Sigurd's father was near death so Sigurd and Gullveig took Agnar and set sail with great haste. Sigurd piled on the sails so the boat would make good time, taking no rest for himself and staying on deck to encourage the sailors to keep up speed. But eventually he could not stay awake a moment longer so he went below and lay down, leaving Gullveig and Agnar on deck.

He was not long gone before Gullveig saw a black boat sailing over the horizon. As it came nearer, she could see the boat was made of stone, with only one person onboard. The stone boat drew alongside and the most dreadfully ugly witch clambered up beside the princess. In her terror, Gullveig became as stone herself, quite unable to move or cry out. The witch took hold of her and pulled off all her fine clothes which she then put on herself. Covering Gullveig with a dirty old cloak, the witch pushed her into the stone boat and, with a shove, set the boat sailing back from whence it came. Before long, the boat was quite out of sight.

As soon as the stone boat was no longer visible, Agnar began to cry. The witch tried to hush the baby but he just kept on wailing and in the end Sigurd awoke and came up on deck to see what was the matter. The witch had taken on a human form so Sigurd did not notice anything amiss, although he was astonished when the supposed princess spoke to him in great anger, complaining that Sigurd should not have left her alone. She had never raised her voice to him before, but he was so busy trying to calm Agnar that he thought no more of it.

When they finally sailed into port it was to be greeted with the sad news that the old king had died. Sigurd was crowned king in his place and he set about restoring his kingdom to happiness. All went well, except that Agnar hardly ever stopped crying from morn to night, though he had been such a good child before. Sigurd decided the child needed a nurse and as soon as she took over looking after him, Agnar stopped crying.

After a while, it seemed to Sigurd that his princess, who was now the queen of course, had changed towards him since the voyage. He began to think that perhaps he had not made such a good choice of wife after all. She was always grumpy and spiteful, and spent a great deal of time locked away in her own room.

The nurse looked after Agnar as though he were her own and she could not help but notice that the boy always cried whenever the queen was near. But she kept quiet about this.

Then, one evening, as she was putting Agnar to bed, there was a flash of pure white light and a great hole opened up in the floor. A beautiful woman, dressed all in gold, with a great iron chain round her waist, rose up through the hole, took Agnar in her arms and covered him with kisses, tears falling down her face all the while. Then she sank back through the floor which closed up

behind her. The nurse was very frightened but did not dare say anything about this strange occurrence in case people thought she was not fit to look after Agnar.

The very next evening, the same thing happened. But this time the beautiful woman spoke as she held Agnar in her arms. "Two are gone, and only one is left," she sighed sadly, then the floor closed over her again.

This time, the nurse felt she could not keep these events secret so she went to the king and told him all that had happened. He trusted her completely and believed her strange tale. The next evening, he joined the nurse and Agnar in the nursery, his sword drawn in his hand. Soon, the white light filled the room again and as the beautiful woman came up through the floor, Sigurd could see that it was his own dear wife. He leapt to her side, severed the iron chain round her waist and caught her in his arms. There was a great rattling sound as the iron chain fell through the floor and seemed to tumble over and over again through the darkness. Agnar laughed with delight.

Gullveig told Sigurd the whole terrible story of how the witch had sailed up in the stone boat and taken her place. The stone boat had sailed through the darkness until it reached the gates of a huge stone castle where a three-

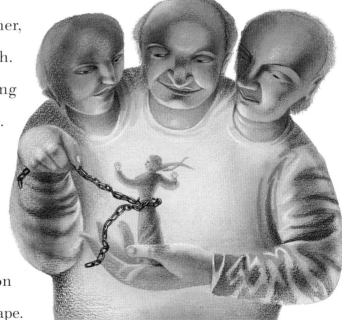

headed giant had taken her prisoner, demanding that she marry him forthwith. She refused over and over again, plotting all the while how she might escape. Eventually, she promised the three-headed giant that she would indeed marry him if he would only let her return for three nights to see her son Agnar first. The giant agreed, but had tied the great iron chain round her waist so she could not escape.

The king now understood why his supposed queen had been so bad-tempered, and he ordered that she be brought into the nursery immediately. No longer in the guise of his beautiful wife, the witch stood spitting and scratching in front of everyone, and then with a great cry she flung herself through the floor after the iron chain. And she was never seen again in all the land. The king and queen ruled for many years in great happiness and Agnar grew up to become a fine young man – who always took special care of his mother.

Don Giovanni de la Fortuna

A SICILIAN FOLK TALE

There was once a wealthy young Sicilian man whose name was Don Giovanni de la Fortuna. But with his spendthrift nature he soon used up all his money and, when there was truly not a single gold coin left, he had to give away all his richly brocaded jackets and travel the roads as a beggar. Who knows how long this state of affairs might have lasted but for a chance meeting with a wizard.

Now, the wizard was in league with the devil and together they were looking for souls to buy, so when he heard the young man's story the wizard rubbed his hands in glee for surely he had found another gullible fool.

"I can make you rich beyond your wildest dreams," wheedled the wizard. "I can make you so rich you will never want for anything again," he promised.

Now the young man, you will remember, was a Sicilian and he was not as green as he looked, so he played the wizard along. "That sounds wonderful, but what do I have to give to you in return?" asked Don Giovanni de la Fortuna carefully.

"Oh, nothing really," said the wizard carelessly. "I will give you this magic purse and all you have to do is say 'My dear purse, I need some money' and it will fill your hands until you tell it to stop."

"Marvellous!" said the young man and he held out his hand for the purse.

"Oh, there's something else I should just mention," grinned the wizard. "You must not wash yourself, comb your hair or shave your beard, or even change your clothes for three years, three months and three days for the magic to work. If you do all this, the purse will be yours forever."

The wizard expected the young man to turn away at such a prospect, but Don Giovanni was made of stronger stuff. He took the purse firmly in his hand and saluted the wizard before striding away.

The purse lived up to all expectations and soon Don Giovanni was a wealthy young man again. But, of course, he was also not an especially nice young man to be near. After a while his hair was matted and tangled, his beard was almost down to his knees, his clothes were disgusting (and very smelly) and worst of all – he had fleas! But he didn't care; his tatty pockets were full of gold coins.

Now one morning, he was passing an especially fine villa. The sun glittered off the polished marble courtyard and the fountains were sparkling and huge pots of exotic flowers filled the air with their heady perfume. Don Giovanni picked off some of his fleas as he sat on the steps, listening to the bees buzzing as they crammed themselves into the flowers. But before long, the master of the house came out and shouted at him from a careful distance downwind, "Go away, you filthy beggar! You smell disgusting and my house will be overrun with fleas!"

"There is no call for you to be so rude," retorted Don Giovanni hotly. "I am no beggar. Why, I could buy this villa from you ten times over!"

Now the owner of the house thought this a huge joke, so he called out, "I shall fetch my lawyer immediately and have him draw up the sale contract."

He thought this would frighten the beggar away but, as we know, Don Giovanni de la Fortuna was made of stronger stuff. So when the lawyer drew up the contract, Don Giovanni promised to return the next day with the money. He went to the local inn and locked himself in a room with the magic purse. The room was soon so full of gold coins that Don Giovanni had difficulty finding room to lie down to sleep.

The next day, he presented himself at the villa, riding on a cart piled high with bags and bags of gold. A contract is a contract, especially to a Sicilian, so soon the villa was his and there he lived, getting smellier by the day.

One year passed, then two and then three. Soon, Don Giovanni would have met the wizard's demands, and he could enjoy the rest of his life. But life is never as easy as that. Word of Don Giovanni's huge fortune had reached the ears of the king, who was always fighting battles and so needed great wealth to pay his soldiers. The king sent a message to Don Giovanni, asking if he might borrow a large sum of money.

You can imagine the king's astonishment when a huge wagon arrived at the palace, laden with even more gold than he had asked for. The king took what he required and sent the rest back. But Don Giovanni refused to accept it, saying he did not need such a handful of gold. The king was even more astonished and spoke to the queen.

"This Don Giovanni is obviously not only wealthy beyond all imagination, he is clearly also a gentleman. I would like to offer him the hand of our elder daughter in marriage."

(That was how these things were arranged in those days.)

Don Giovanni was delighted. Things were turning out extraordinarily well for him. The king requested a portrait of Don Giovanni so the princess could see her future husband, and this was sent back to the palace along with Don Giovanni's acceptance of the marriage proposal. But when the princess saw the portrait, she screamed and fell down in a faint. The queen held some smelling salts under her nose but then she saw the portrait too. She shouted at the king, "Our daughter can never marry such a filthy, horrible-looking beggar!"

"But, my dear, how was I to know Don Giovanni would look like that? I have given my royal word, the wedding must go ahead."

The princess screamed and tore her hair and drummed her heels on the carpet. "I will never, ever marry that repulsive creature!"

Then a quiet voice spoke. It was the younger princess, who was a great deal less spoiled than her elder sister. "My father, of course you must keep your word. I will marry Don Giovanni de la Fortuna. Who knows, I might even be able to persuade him to have a bath now and again."

So it was settled. The king was happy; the queen thought her younger child had quite taken leave of her senses; the elder princess mocked her sister every day; and, of course, Don Giovanni was delighted for it seemed to him one princess would be as good as another.

Then, to complete his happiness, the three years, three months and three days were up. The wizard appeared suddenly on the morning of the fourth day, and he was not in a good humour. Not only had he lost his magic purse, but he had no soul to offer the devil. But a contract is a contract, especially to a Sicilian, so he had to release Don Giovanni de la Fortuna from his filthy state.

You can imagine the preparations then! Don Giovanni hired the best barber and the best tailor in all the land. He had twenty baths one day and another twenty the next. He used enough soap to wash an entire army and poured endless flagons of expensive bath oil into the water. Then, in his splendid new clothes, he set off for the palace with a great retinue of servants and musicians, the grumbling wizard following at a distance.

The younger princess smiled quietly when she realized the handsome young man was Don Giovanni de la Fortuna. Her elder sister, however, was so angry that she worked herself up into a towering rage and expired from sheer bad temper. And so the wizard was pleased too, for he had a soul to give to the devil after all. Don Giovanni de la Fortuna gave up his spendthrift ways and when the king died he ruled in his place. No one in the land ever wanted for anything ever again, as Don Giovanni shared the good fortune of the magic purse with everyone from his lovely princess to the thinnest farm cat.

The Crystal Cabinets

A TALE OF TRANSFORMATION FROM OLD GERMANY

Gervaise the young tailor decided one day that he had spent enough time sitting in his dark workroom stitching, endlessly stitching, so he closed the shutters and set off on his travels. He strode out of the city gates and through meadows and over rivers, his heart lifting at every step. He felt free for the first time in his short life.

As dusk fell, Gervaise found himself in an ancient forest. Great spreading oak trees shaded the grass and wild boar rootled for acorns. Gervaise spent the night on a bed of springy moss, within the sound of a running brook. He was woken abruptly the following morning by the sounds of a huge struggle.

The ground shuddered as branches cracked and fell from the trees, and in the background some beast was roaring and stamping the ground. Gervaise scrambled to his feet and peered round the tree he had been sleeping under. In a clearing, he saw a fine stag with a great head of antlers charging a coal-black bull again and again. The bull was snorting and bellowing, but Gervaise could see that the stag was winning the battle and, even as he stepped out for a closer look, the bull sank to its feet and did not rise again.

The stag flung back its mighty head and roared in triumph, and then charged right up to Gervaise. It tossed him up onto its back and galloped off through the forest, never pausing in its flight. Over hills and through valleys, splashing across rivers and rushing across meadows, Gervaise clung on for dear life all the while, his eyes tightly shut. And then, the headlong flight stopped as suddenly as it had started. His knees trembling, Gervaise slid off the stag's back and lay on the ground to recover.

Gervaise found himself lying in front of a sheer wall of rock. A cold wind was blowing. Of the stag, there was absolutely no sign whatsoever. Then a quiet voice spoke, "Have no fear, Gervaise. No harm shall come to you if you do as I say."

Gervaise looked around. There was no one to be seen.

"There is a door in the rock face in front of you. Enter and good luck will be yours," urged the voice.

Gervaise scrambled to his feet. As he looked at the forbidding cliff he saw there was indeed a door cut out of the rock. It was carved with all kinds of ornate beasts and plants — and it was slightly ajar. He stepped inside cautiously. He found himself in a vast lofty chamber, roughly hewn out of the rock. The floor was covered in richly coloured marble tiles, and large tapestries covered the walls. He walked further in, his footsteps echoing on the tiles. Against the far wall, Gervaise could see two great crystal cabinets, lit from below by a smoky blue light. He tiptoed closer, afraid to disturb some ancient magic if he made a sound. He peered into the first cabinet and held his breath in wonderment.

The cabinet contained the most perfect miniature model of a great castle surrounded by barns and stables and fields of corn. With a start, Gervaise realized the corn was waving and everywhere little figures were going about their business. The shepherd was rounding up the sheep and the stable boys were brushing the horses in their stalls till their coats gleamed. Gervaise peered closer through the tiny windows, at the cooks bustling in and out of the hot kitchens. He saw a clerk entering columns of figures in a weighty ledger, a butler polishing a great silver teapot and the housekeeper piling freshly laundered sheets into a deep press.

The quiet voice spoke again. "Turn around, Gervaise, and look into the other cabinet, and you shall see what you shall see."

Gervaise did as he was bid and his heart thudded in his chest so loudly that he felt it must echo through the entire chamber. For there, asleep in the second cabinet, lay the most beautiful young girl. Her hair was as dark as the raven's wing and her cheeks as fair as the softest snowfall. She wore a green silk dress, and in her hand she clasped a pair of richly embroidered hunting gloves.

"Push back the bolt in front of the cabinet," said the voice.

With trembling fingers Gervaise did as he was bid. The lid creaked up. The girl's eyes flew open. They were the deepest emerald green.

"At last! I am free from this awful crystal prison," she cried, and Gervaise took her hand to help her down from the cabinet. As soon as her feet touched the ground, she whirled round and slammed the lid of the cabinet shut. "Young man, you have saved my life. Now I have an even greater task for you. But first I must tell you my story."

Gervaise spread his cloak on the floor and the young girl sat down gracefully, beckoning him to join her.

"My name is Belinda and I am the daughter of a wealthy merchant. My parents died when I was very young but I was fortunate to have an older brother, Roland, who looked after me and brought me up as our parents would have wished. We were happy together, so much so that we had resolved never to marry anyone but to look after each other all the days of our lives. We lived in a splendid castle and we had many friends – for we always kept open house for those less fortunate than ourselves. But one terrible evening our contentment was shattered," and here Belinda's eyes filled with tears.

Gervaise scrabbled in his pocket and produced a rather grubby handkerchief, but Belinda just sniffed loudly and continued with her tale.

"It was an evening in winter. The winds were battering the walls of the castle and the rain was pouring down the gutters. There was a knock at the door and there stood a stranger who claimed to be lost. We welcomed him in, of course, and Roland seemed to take to him immediately. But there was something about him that I did not trust. He was dressed all in purple and his eyes glittered darkly whenever he looked at me. I so disliked him that I retired early to my chambers and took up my embroidery to calm my heart, which was greatly disquieted by our visitor. You can imagine my distress when he suddenly appeared by my side despite the door being firmly bolted. I demanded that he leave instantly but he only laughed, and it was not a nice sound."

81

At this, Gervaise was already on his feet, demanding that Belinda lead him to this sinister stranger that he might be taught a lesson. Belinda held his arm and said softly, "There is worse to come. The stranger revealed that he was a powerful magician and he wished me to marry him forthwith! I rejected him in no uncertain terms, you may be sure. But he was greatly angered by my refusal and, as he strode out of the room, promised me that he would have his revenge. I passed the night in great fear and as soon as it was daylight I ran to my brother's room to tell him all that had passed. But he was not to be found. My heart grew heavy as I searched the castle, and all my worst fears were realized when the groom told me that Roland had gone hunting with the magician at daybreak.

"I galloped off in pursuit and before long I saw the magician coming towards me, leading a great stag. But of my brother, there was no sign. I asked the magician where Roland was and why he was leading the stag, whose eyes I saw were filled with tears. And then I realized. The magician had transformed Roland into the stag. Before I even had time to speak my fears,

the magician threw some coloured dust in my eyes and I knew no more. When I awoke I was here in this chamber, lying in the crystal cabinet. The magician appeared by my side and told me he had indeed turned Roland into a stag, and he had also transported our castle into the other crystal cabinet. If I was still unwilling to be his bride then I would remain here for ever and ever. And here I have been until you appeared," said Belinda.

"Well, I think your brother brought me here," cried Gervaise in delight. "Now all we have to do is find a way of restoring you both to your castle and Roland to his human form." And Gervaise explained to an increasingly joyful Belinda that it was a huge stag that had led him to her side.

Gervaise carried the crystal cabinet very carefully out of the rocky chamber and, just as he passed through the carved door, the cabinet shattered and the castle began miraculously to grow to its proper size. The stables and the barns and all the people too – all were restored.

"Welcome to my home!" laughed Belinda, and she led the overwhelmed Gervaise through the magnificent terraced gardens and across the bustling courtyard, up into the great hall. A figure stood by the huge fireplace at the far end of the room – it was Roland! He and Belinda hugged each other, both crying with happiness, and then they hugged some more. Roland explained that he had indeed been the stag fighting with the coal-black bull who was none other than the wicked magician in one of his many disguises. As the stag, he had mortally wounded the bull, and so the magician would trouble them no longer.

And so it was, from that day forth, that everyone lived happily ever after in the safely restored castle. Roland and Belinda were still very hospitable to all their friends, but they were a little more wary of strangers. They invited Gervaise to come and live with them in the castle and, for all you know, he might be there still!

Merlin, the Greatest Wizard of Them All

A GREAT LEGEND FROM ENGLAND

Gorlois, the Duke of Cornwall, paced the cold stone battlements of Tintagel Castle. It was a wild night. Huge seas crashed at the foot of the cliffs, the boom of the waves echoing up to where the duke strode restlessly, buffeted by the soaking rain and the mighty winds that roared about his head. The fierceness of the wind and rain matched the anger that raged in his heart. Now the duke had a wife, the Lady Igraine, who was renowned through the length and breadth of Cornwall for her beauty. She loved and honoured her husband, but her beauty had not escaped the notice of the king, Uther Pendragon. Uther wanted Lady Igraine to leave Gorlois and become his wife instead. Gorlois knew what was in the king's heart, and he feared for his lady.

And now, Uther had shown his hand. His great army lay encamped beneath the castle walls, and Gorlois knew he had a mighty battle on his hands in the morning.

Great fires burned in a circle round the walls and Gorlois could see row upon row of soldiers lining up in readiness. They seemed remarkably well organized and disciplined – and there were a great number of them. He turned on his heel, despair filling his thoughts, and walked back into the great hall where the Lady Igraine sat huddled by the huge fireplace.

"I must go and fight, my Lady. For your honour, and mine," and Gorlois looked closely at the Lady Igraine. "The king is determined in this," he whispered.

"I shall never, ever marry Uther Pendragon!" Lady Igraine declared. "Whether you live or die, my Lord, my heart is forever yours," and she smiled at Gorlois. "Be of good cheer, you will win tomorrow. Uther Pendragon has many enemies and he will not have it all his own way."

But Lady Igraine's brave words were blown far out to sea the next day as the fierce battle raged. Gorlois was killed along with most of his men, fighting by his side. The Lady Igraine was filled with profound grief and a burning anger, and refused to speak to Uther Pendragon when he strode, still bloody and dishevelled, into the great hall after the battle. He and his soldiers stayed for several days, eating and carousing far into the night, but from the Lady Igraine, barricaded in her rooms, there came no word of surrender or welcome. The king was not used to being so defied and he realized his infatuation was making him look foolish, so he took his soldiers and departed, but he shouted over his shoulder as he left that the Lady Igraine must think to her future. She realized then that he was never going to give up his attempts to persuade her to become his wife. Her anger and despair hardened into an icy resolve.

Now Britain at this time was a wild and lawless place. Enchanters practised their evil arts, and wizards wove magic spells to bend people to their will. The greatest of these wizards was Merlin. He would appear as if by magic (as it no doubt was) and disappear with equal suddenness. Merlin had long been an advisor to Uther, and indeed he had predicted that Uther's son and heir would be a great king who would follow in his father's footsteps.

So Uther summoned Merlin. "If I am to have this great son that you keep predicting, I must have a wife!" he bellowed. "There is only one lady I wish to be my wife and that is the fair Lady Igraine, but in her heart there burns a deep hatred for me."

"One year after you marry Lady Igraine you will have a son. He will become the greatest king Britain has ever known. But I must be the one to raise him," cautioned Merlin. "The moment he is born, you must give him to me and I will see to it that he is taken care of until such time as he is ready to prove himself."

Uther Pendragon heard nothing of this other than the prediction that he would marry the Lady Igraine.

"Tush, Merlin! You talk in riddles," he muttered. "I care not if you take the child. But use your magic to make the Lady Igraine love me."

"Promise me the child first," said Merlin fiercely.

"I promise," said the king. The promise meant nothing to Uther and in the morning he had forgotten all about it. But Merlin kept his word and, the next time Uther Pendragon went to Tintagel Castle, he was astonished to receive a warm welcome from Lady Igraine. Within a very short while they were married and it was as if poor Gorlois had never existed, so great and deep were the enchantments of Merlin.

A year after they were married, Lady Igraine gave birth to a son. He was given the name Arthur. Uther was busy preparing for another battle even as his child was born. Lady Igraine and Uther Pendragon may have forgotten Gorlois under the enchantments of Merlin, but many of the lords and barons had not. They felt little love for Uther Pendragon who had ridden roughshod over them in his attempts to gain total power in the land.

When Uther came into the inner chamber to inspect his baby, he found the Lady Igraine in a deep sleep and Merlin standing by the cradle. Something in his countenance chilled Uther to the depths of his heart.

"I have come for the child," growled Merlin. "You have surely not forgotten your promise?"

"I was not thinking straight when I made that foolish promise," laughed Uther nervously. "I want my son to grow up here by my side. I must school him in the ways of a great ruler. I cannot have him running wild with some magician."

Merlin's face darkened with anger. "I will have the boy!" he commanded. "If he stays here he will die."

Then Uther realized what Merlin was saying. Uther would not win his battle with the restless barons and he himself would die. He thrust the sleeping baby into Merlin's arms and turned away to hide the fear that was in his eyes.

The very next day, Uther Pendragon met his death on the battlefield.

Merlin took the baby to a noble knight, Sir Ector, who was not caught up in all the feuding and the danger that surrounded the king. Sir Ector had a son, Kay, and young Arthur grew up as his squire, knowing nothing of his true origins. Merlin kept an eye on him from a distance, but did nothing to interfere with his upbringing and education.

Civil war raged throughout Britain for sixteen years after the death of Uther Pendragon. Villages were razed to the ground, towns were under seige for months on end and crops rotted in the ground, as there were no men left on the land to bring in the harvest. Eventually, even the great warlords were battle-weary and they all met in Canterbury Cathedral to resolve their disputes and to choose a new king. Many were the arguments as tempers flared and peace seemed as far distant a possibility as ever, when a fierce voice echoed round the cloisters.

"Enough! You will never be able to make a lasting peace if you cannot even agree among yourselves."

Everyone turned to look into the deep shadows from where the voice came. Dark eyes glittered in the gloom and then Merlin himself stood before them, his dark robes swirling round his feet so that he looked like a huge crow.

"Come outside," he commanded, "and see what I have devised with my magic art to find your next king."

Everyone crowded outside in the courtyard and there, four foot square, stood a huge marble stone. On top of it was placed a heavy iron anvil, and sunk deep in the anvil was a sword, glittering strangely. The sword was finely wrought and the hilt was chased in silver. On the marble there gleamed in carved gold letters the words:

Whosoever pulleth

out the sword

from the anvil

is the true-born

great King of England.

Needless to say, every single one of the lords pushed forward to prove their claim to be the rightful king. But not one was able to move the sword the merest inch. Merlin looked on, unsmiling and grim.

Finally he spoke, "Go back to your castles, every one of you. The great King of England is not standing here today. But on New Year's Day, at the jousting tournament, someone will pull the sword from the anvil – he will be your king!"

News of the tournament reached Sir Ector's castle. Kay was determined to try his hand at the contest, and so he set off, Arthur by his side. Kay was a brave champion and fought like a lion, but in one fierce clash his sword was broken.

"Arthur!" he cried, "You must find me another sword so I may continue! I have to try to win the tournament."

Arthur had no idea where he might find another sword, but he dashed off straight away. He kept bumping into people, ducking and diving until he found himself in a quiet courtyard beside the cathedral. The sound of his feet rang round the old stone walls. Then his eyes lit up. There, in the centre of the courtyard, was a sword thrust deep in the heart of a great iron anvil. Arthur did not pause. He grasped the sword and pulled. The sword slid out of the anvil, the metal ringing in the silence. Arthur shouted in delight and dashed back to the tournament.

But when Kay saw the sword in Arthur's hand, he grew pale. The crowds around Arthur drew back, fear in their eyes.

"Where did you get that sword, boy?" whispered Sir Ector.

"I found it in a courtyard near here, in an anvil…" his voice trailed off.

Everyone started talking at once. The babble rose to a crescendo, then faded away as a voice was heard over all the hubbub.

"I give you Arthur, the true-born great King of England!"

It was Merlin, appearing as if by magic once again. He led Arthur back to the anvil and made him read the inscription. Then Merlin sat down with Arthur and told him exactly who he was. They talked long into the night, long after the excited crowds had dispersed, long after the great lords had knelt to pledge their allegiance to the new king.

And thereafter, Arthur's life was intertwined with Merlin's for the rest of his days — Merlin, the greatest wizard of them all.